for Tony — J.W.
for Jeanne — T.R.

Text copyright © 1998 by Jeanne Willis. Illustrations copyright © 1998 by Tony Ross.
The rights of Jeanne Willis and Tony Ross to be identified as the author and illustrator of this work
have been asserted by them in accordance with the Copyright, Designs and Patents Act, 1988.

First published in Great Britain in 1998 by Andersen Press Ltd., 20 Vauxhall Bridge Road, London SW1V 2SA.
Published in Australia by Random House Australia Pty., 20 Alfred Street, Milsons Point, Sydney, NSW 2061.
All rights reserved. Colour separated in Italy by Fotoriproduzione Grafiche, Verona.
Printed and bound in Italy by Grafiche AZ, Verona.

10   9   8   7   6   5   4   3   2   1

British Library Cataloguing in Publication Data available.

ISBN 0 86264 782 7

This book has been printed on acid-free paper

The Wind in the Wallows

Jeanne Willis + Tony Ross

Andersen Press • London

Under the willows on lily pad pillows
The Swans lay asleep in the stream.

Nothing was stirring except for the whirring
Of Dragonflies' wings in a dream.

The snoring of Newts in their freckly suits
Was as soft as a Duckling's fluff.

In silence, a Butterfly stirred in its sleep
On a duvet of dandelion puff.

Then, **Bang!** And then **Pop!** And then **Poop**! And then **Parp!**
The Pike was the first to awake.

"Was that you?" he accused. "Wasn't me!" said the Carp.
"You have made the most dreadful mistake."

"Then what are those bubbles?" a Trout said. "They trouble
Me. Did they come out of your mouth?"

"In defence of my friend," said a Tadpole, "the end
That they blew from was North,

and not South."

"What a stink! What a stench!" said a little green Tench,
"It is more than a creature can bear.

I am ill to the gills, I need oxygen pills,
Let me through, I must come up for air."

"The Cows on the bank must be playing a prank,"
Said a Rat. "It is rank, it is wrong."

"Us?" the Cows fussed. "It's the Sheep you can't trust.
It is them that's creating the pong."

"No need to get sniffy," the Sheep said, "it's whiffy,
  We know, but it comes from elsewhere.

We have been clipped. We've been dagged. We've been dipped.
It's that smelly old Fox, over there."

Then **Parp** and then **Poop**! And then **Poot!** And then **Boop!**

"That noise," said the Fox, "is the Owls.
They're always the same after gorging on game,
It does terrible things to their bowels."

"What a thing to imply!" screeched the Owls. "We deny
Any part in this stinking affair.

A word to the wise — they've escaped from their sties,
Several Pigs. Which explains the bad air."

"They must go," huffed the Horse and the Hare said, "Of course,
I suspected the Swine all along.

The smell of the country is all very well
In small doses. But this is too strong!"

"Let's flush them out!" said the Shrew with a shout,
And so down to the wallows they went.

But no Pigs could be seen . . .

. . . just a Boy dressed in green,
With a big tin of beans
and a tent.